★ CELEBRITY ACTIVISTS ★

CHILDREN'S CAUSES

KATHY KATELLA-COFRANCESCO

Youth Middle School
Media Center

Twenty-First Century Books

Brookfield, Connecticut

Twenty-First Century Books
A Division of The Millbrook Press
2 Old New Milford Road
Brookfield, CT 06804

©1998 by Blackbirch Graphics, Inc.
First Edition
5 4 3 2 1

Printed in the United States of America on acid free paper.∞

Created and produced in association with Blackbirch Graphics, Inc.

Library of Congress Cataloging-in-Publication Data

Katella-Cofrancesco, Kathy.
    Children's causes / Kathy Katella-Cofrancesco. — 1st ed.
       p.   cm. — (Celebrity activists)
    Includes bibliographical references and index.
    Summary: Describes the work done by such well-known personalities as Dave
Thomas, Shaquille O'Neal, Mariah Carey, and Jackie Joyner-Kersee to raise money
for organizations that make a difference in the lives of children.
    ISBN 0-7613-3013-5 (alk. paper)
    1. Children—Services for—Juvenile literature. 2. Children—Services for—United
States—Juvenile literature. 3. Volunteer workers in social service—United States—
Juvenile literature. 4. Celebrities—United States—Charitable contributions—Juvenile
literature. 5. Fund raisers (Persons)—United States—Juvenile literature. [1. Celebrities.
2. Child welfare.] I. Title. II. Series.
HV713.K37   1998
361.7'0973—dc21
                                                   97-38924
                                                      CIP
                                                       AC

CONTENTS

INTRODUCTION

One of our finest American traditions is philanthropy—giving of ourselves, by either donating time or money, to those who need us. Helping the less fortunate is part of our heritage and is a quality that we can be proud of.

For many people who are very well known to the public, this sense of responsibility toward others is especially strong. Successful athletes, actors, musicians, business leaders, and others often accept their positions in the spotlight as role models, and they look for opportunities to give something back to their communities. These celebrities play important roles in helping charitable groups educate the public and raise money for a variety of causes. When a favorite baseball player or movie star asks people for their help in benefiting a cause, chances are good that people are going to listen to the message and want to show their support.

There are thousands of nonprofit organizations in the United States that are working to improve our quality of life—whether it is by ending hunger and child abuse, protecting the environment, increasing literacy and educational opportunities, or helping to provide treatments and find cures for diseases.

In 1989, I established the Celebrity Outreach Foundation to help charitable groups enlist the help of celebrities who support their causes and are looking for opportunities to help. It was the first organization of its kind in the country. To date, we have matched more than 600 celebrities with 350 nonprofit organizations.

Before we could help anyone, however, we had to establish our own credibility as a new foundation. Gregory Peck, Whoopi Goldberg, Dan Aykroyd, Eddie Murphy, Alec Baldwin, Tony Danza, and others stepped forward to support our efforts. A Celebrity Advisory Committee was formed. The names of all the committee members are featured in our promotion materials. Without the committee's support, it would have been much more difficult to establish our identity.

The celebrities featured in this book have all made major commitments by contributing their time, money, and names to help a variety of causes. (There are many others, but unfortunately we do not have the space to include every philanthropic celebrity.) Their efforts have made a significant difference in the lives of many people.

Bob Oettinger
Celebrity Outreach Foundation

HELPING TROUBLED FAMILIES

Many actors, athletes, and other celebrities go out of their way to help children who are underprivileged, orphaned, or abused. They are powerful spokespersons who can make a major difference in the lives of these children. Because people recognize these celebrities, their involvement draws attention to the problems children face. They are able to educate people about issues affecting children, make public service announcements, and raise millions of dollars hosting fund-raising activities. Some of these celebrities have also started foundations—organizations that distribute money and help to a particular cause—to benefit children who live in the cities and towns where they grew up.

Kevin Spacey ★

Kevin Spacey is an actor who has played many different roles—from drunks and gangsters to Clarence Darrow, the famous criminal defense lawyer. He won an Academy Award for his supporting role in a movie called *The Usual Suspects*, and a Tony Award for his work in a play titled *Lost in Yonkers*. Spacey has also received honors from the Screen Actors Guild and the New York Film Critics.

For Spacey, however, one of his most important roles is as a supporter of the Greenwich House Children's Safety Project, a child abuse prevention program in New York City's Greenwich Village. Spacey, who lives in Greenwich Village, learned about the project from a friend who volunteers there.

In 1995, Spacey decided that he would volunteer to help organize the annual Teddy Bear Auction—an event that began in 1992 and raises thousands of dollars for the project each year. The auction features teddy bears that have been personalized by celebrities. People bid on each bear and the person who is willing to pay the most money gets to keep it. Actors have dressed bears in costumes similar to the ones they wore in movie roles, and singers have attached their latest CDs to the bears.

Kevin Spacey displays one of the bears auctioned off at the 1996 Teddy Bear Auction, which raised money for the Greenwich House Children's Safety Project.

In 1996, Natalie Merchant made two bears and Madonna dressed a teddy bear in a leather jacket that looked like the one she wore on a concert tour.

Months before the auction takes place, Spacey contacts celebrities and asks them to donate bears or funds for the project. He even helps set up the auction before it starts.

Spacey has co-hosted the auction for two years. In 1995, he co-hosted with actress Susan Sarandon, and in 1996 with talk show host Rosie O'Donnell. One year, drawing on his theatrical imagination, Spacey dressed *himself* up as a teddy bear. The auction raised $150,000 that year, which included $6,000 for a bear from Sesame Street and $500 for Spacey's costume.

When asked why he thinks the Teddy Bear Auction is a logical way to support children, Spacey told *US* magazine that, "Teddy bears are a symbol of what makes kids safe."

The money raised for Greenwich House at each Teddy Bear Auction is put to good use. The organization was founded by Mary Kingsbury Simkhovitch on Thanksgiving Day in 1902.

Its mission is to improve the quality of life of people living in New York City. Greenwich House has programs that help children, the elderly, and people coping with problems that range from alcohol and drug abuse to living with AIDS.

There are 50,000 cases of child abuse reported in New York City every year, and the Greenwich House Children's Safety Project opens its doors to families who need assistance. The project provides counseling and other services for children and families of children who have been physically or sexually abused, or who have witnessed a crime—including domestic violence.

The project also conducts Saturday Safety Classes in which children who are five and older are taught how to protect themselves, including what to do if someone they know or love is hurting them, how to get help, how to identify and avoid dangerous situations, how to distinguish between a good and a bad touch, and how to assert themselves if somebody touches them in the wrong way.

In addition to his work for the auctions, Spacey has also recorded Children's Safety Project public service announcements that are aired on a New York radio station. These announcements educate children about the different ways they can protect themselves.

While he is one celebrity who doesn't talk much about his off-screen life, Spacey doesn't mind speaking out about the Children's Safety Project. His work has inspired other celebrities to get involved with this organization, including Christian Slater, Whoopi Goldberg, Ellen Barkin, Robert DeNiro, Paul Newman, Oprah Winfrey, David Letterman, Anne Klein, and several of the New York Rangers. Kevin Spacey is an excellent example of how one person's efforts can cause a positive chain reaction.

★ *Childhelp USA* ★

Kathleen Turner has played major roles in the theater and in such hit movies as *Peggy Sue Got Married, Serial Mom,* and *Romancing the Stone.* She was also the voice of Jessica Rabbit in *Who Framed Roger Rabbit?*

Turner has developed a reputation for speaking out about things that she doesn't agree with. As a mother, she gets especially angry when she sees children suffer. So, in 1994, she decided to become involved, helping children in need through a nonprofit organization called Childhelp USA.

Childhelp USA was founded by Sara O'Meara and Yvonne Fedderson, two actresses who met in the 1950s on a television program called the "Ozzie and Harriet Show." During a goodwill tour to entertain American soldiers stationed in Japan, O'Meara and Fedderson saw homeless and abandoned children wandering the streets of Tokyo. Most of them were Amerasians—children of both Asian and American descent—who were orphaned or abandoned by their parents. The two women worked to organize the funding, construction, and operation of nine orphanages in Japan.

O'Meara and Fedderson founded International Orphans, Inc. (IOI) in 1959. In 1966, the U.S. government asked the two women to help orphaned victims of the Vietnam War. IOI built and maintained five orphanages, a hospital, and a school in Vietnam. And in 1975, after the fall of Saigon (when the capital of South Vietnam, Saigon, was taken over by the North Vietnamese), IOI helped to organize "Baby Lifts," bringing thousands of Vietnamese orphans to America for adoption.

In 1996, Kathleen Turner addressed the National Press Club on behalf of Childhelp.

The two actresses also recognized that there are children in this country who are in need of help, so, in 1983, they shifted the focus of their efforts and renamed the group Childhelp USA. Currently, the organization operates the Childhelp National Child Abuse Hotline (1-800-4-A-CHILD®), two residential treatment facilities (places where children can recover from the experience of child abuse), foster and group homes, two advocacy/diagnostic centers for sexually abused children, and numerous community outreach and education programs across the country.

Turner has dedicated herself to educating people about Childhelp's mission. As a celebrity, she feels she can persuade more people to listen to her. "I can get attention to the organization and get volunteers involved," she said at a Childhelp banquet in 1996. That same year, Turner also addressed the National Press Club in Washington, D.C. She said, "More than three children die every day as a result of child abuse or neglect. Ending carnage of this magnitude requires every one of us to become involved. Unless each one of us makes a commitment to do all we can to help, children remain in serious danger." Turner has also participated in Childhelp fund-raisers in New York City; Richmond, Virginia; and Washington, D.C., and has appeared in a Childhelp informational video.

Other celebrities have also pitched in for Childhelp USA. In 1990, Jane Seymour, star of "Dr. Quinn, Medicine Woman" and several Childhelp informational videos, was named "Woman of the World" by the organization. This is an honor Childhelp has been bestowing for more than 35 years on women who have made a positive impact on children and humanity in general. In addition, as spokesperson for Clairol Loving Care, Seymour got that company involved in a project in which Clairol donated 50 cents from the sale of every box of Loving Care sold in April 1997–up to $25,000. Seymour has also donated several of her own watercolor paintings for fund-raising auctions. And each year, actor and musician John Stamos, who starred in "Full House," hosts the Christmas Program at Village of Childhelp West–the nation's first residential treatment program exclusively for severely abused children.

Kathleen Turner appreciates the chance Childhelp gives her to help others. "I'm very old-fashioned in some ways because of my father, who thought that being a public servant was an honor," she said in a 1995 article in *Interview* magazine. "Everyone must find a capacity in which they can serve, because we all benefit from society. You shouldn't get to live in society and give nothing back."

Andre Agassi ★

Andre Agassi is one of the best tennis players in the world. The winner of a gold medal in the 1996 Olympic Games, he has also been a champion in major tournaments, including the Australian Open, the U.S. Open, and Wimbledon. He often competes with his friend and rival, Pete Sampras, for the honor of being the game's top athlete.

Agassi has also won respect for changing his attitude toward his sport. After years of letting the pressure to win make him nervous, he decided to be less intense and to really enjoy what he was doing. Agassi also wanted to branch out from thinking only of tennis and felt a strong pull to help needy children. In 1994, the athlete started the Andre Agassi Foundation to provide educational and recreational opportunities for kids living in Las Vegas, Nevada, where he grew up.

In the last few years, the foundation has raised millions of dollars to help fund programs for children. Some of the money comes from the annual Andre Agassi Grand Slam for Children fund-raiser—a celebrity gala, auction, and concert. Other celebrities have volunteered to help with the event, including Arnold Schwarzenegger, Robin Williams, Bruce Willis, Elton John, Vanessa Williams, and Brooke Shields—Agassi's wife. At one of the auctions, people pledged $50,000 for a chance to appear on Shields's television show, "Suddenly Susan," and $110,000 to have a private dining experience with Emeril Lagasse, a world-famous chef.

Agassi is proud that his foundation is funded almost entirely from his direct contributions and other private donations. This allows it to give most of the money that is raised to organizations that help children. The foundation has provided clothing and personal hygiene packs for needy children through the Assistance League of Las Vegas's Operation School Bell; helped fund activities

Andre Agassi began his trip to the 1996 Olympic Games with a visit to an Atlanta Boys & Girls Club, where Agassi's foundation funded a newly surfaced tennis court.

at the Boys & Girls Club of Las Vegas; and paid for temporary care for abused, neglected, or abandoned children at a shelter called Child Haven.

While the Andre Agassi Foundation's primary purpose is to assist at-risk children in the Las Vegas area, Agassi's travels have led him to help children in other areas as well. One such project was a newly surfaced tennis court at the Salvation Army Donnelly Boys & Girls Club of Metro Atlanta. There, a few days before the 1996 Summer Olympic Games in Atlanta, Agassi visited with the children who would be using the court.

Another cause that Agassi's foundation supports is the Cynthia Bunker Memorial Scholarship Fund. This is a scholarship at the College of Performing Arts at the University of Nevada, Las Vegas, that is given each year to a young person who wants to attend the school and needs financial help. The scholarship is in honor of Cynthia Bunker, a UNLV student and a close friend of Agassi's, who was killed in a car accident.

In 1996, the tennis player received national recognition for his good work when *USA Weekend* magazine gave him its "Most Caring Athlete Award" and $1,000 to benefit his foundation. Explaining why raising money for children is important to him, Andre Agassi says, "I have been very blessed and had many opportunities available to me. Children today face so many obstacles. If I can make a positive impact on at least one child's life, then it has all been worthwhile."

★ *Chris Zorich* ★

Whenever football player Chris Zorich's team, the Chicago Bears, had a home game, he would buy tickets and refreshments for a few kids, and arrange for them to visit Bears' Alley, where they could meet players and get autographs. Then he would join them for a meal at the Planet Hollywood restaurant. This is just one of the many things that Zorich has done to earn his reputation as an outstanding humanitarian athlete.

Zorich grew up on the south side of Chicago. He was an only child and biracial, which made him a target for gangs and bullies. He and his mother Zora had little money and couldn't always afford groceries. "I remember standing in line waiting for food," Zorich says of the experience. "That makes an impression on you when you're a little kid. I promised myself if I was ever able to help others, I would."

Zorich has worked hard to achieve a better life. While he was growing up, he looked for support from family, friends, church, and his coaches—who soon realized that he was a talented athlete. After he graduated from Chicago Vocational High School, he earned a football scholarship to the University of Notre Dame, where he became a three-time All-American. He graduated from Notre Dame in 1991, and was drafted by the Chicago Bears that same year. After his first season, Zorich's teammates selected him for the Brian Piccolo Award. This award is given for courage and effort in the face of extreme circumstances both on and off the field. Zorich scored his first National Football League touchdown against the Dallas Cowboys, Super Bowl champions. In his position in the starting lineup, he averaged more than 100 tackles per season, which placed him among the league's best defensive linemen.

Through his foundation, Chris Zorich brings happiness to underprivileged children in Chicago.

Zorich does most of his charitable work through the Christopher Zorich Foundation, a nonprofit organization that he started in 1993 to honor his mother, who died unexpectedly during his senior year at Notre Dame. She was his role model, raising him on just $250 a month that she received through public assistance. "Besides teaching me to always give my best effort, my mom taught me to help others who are deserving and in need," Zorich tells people. "Without her inspiration, love, and support, I would never have had the opportunity to graduate from Notre Dame and become a Chicago Bear."

The Christopher Zorich Foundation is made up of several programs and activities. Chris Zorich & Friends takes kids from orphanages and residential youth homes to the ballet, the zoo, and shows such as Disney's "Snow White on Ice." The foundation also delivers groceries twice a year to nearly 300 Chicago families, sends flowers and toiletries to battered women's shelters in recognition of Mother's Day, and conducts visits to schools to motivate students. At the schools, Zorich talks to students about overcoming adversity and the importance of following one's dreams.

Together, these programs have helped more than 17,000 people. One of these people is Jose Del Real, the first recipient of the Zora Zorich Scholarship, which pays tuition for two students a year at Notre Dame. "In some ways, his life was like my own," says Zorich, explaining that Del Real also resisted the difficulties of the inner city and worked so hard in school that he finished in the top percentile of his high school graduating class.

Zorich talks often about his childhood and his commitment to helping others, and has been profiled on "The Oprah Winfrey Show," and in *TV Guide*, *Sports Illustrated*, *Reader's Digest*, and *Highlights for Children*. His work has earned him many honors, including the Lions Clubs International's "Humanitarian of the Year" in 1996, and the *Sports Illustrated for Kids* "Good Sport" award in 1994.

Chris Zorich decided to leave the Bears after the 1996 season in order to attend John Marshall Law School in Chicago. But he plans to continue doing good work through his foundation. His philosophy is summed up in the words of his late mother, "Treat the world as you would your family, and you'll be rewarded with loyalty and kindness."

Dave Thomas ★

You may have seen Dave Thomas in commercials for Wendy's, promoting his hamburgers, chili, french fries, and soft drinks. He opened the first Wendy's Old Fashioned Hamburgers in 1969, in Columbus, Ohio, naming it after his eight-year-old daughter, Melinda Lou, whose nickname was "Wendy." Today, there are more than 4,800 Wendy's in the United States, as well as in 34 foreign countries.

What many people don't know about Thomas is that he is also a strong supporter of adoption. In 1992, he founded the Dave Thomas Foundation for Adoption to make adoption easier and more affordable for prospective parents. Thomas helps fund the foundation by donating the profits from the sale of his two books, *Dave's Way*, and *Well Done!*

He uses Wendy's to help promote his cause. Each year, if you eat at one of his restaurants during the month of November, you'll see display posters and tray liners featuring photographs of children who are waiting to be adopted. The toll-free number of the National Adoption Foundation is also displayed prominently.

For Dave Thomas, adoption is an issue that hits close to home. Born in 1932 in Atlantic City, New Jersey, he never knew his birth parents.

In 1995, Dave Thomas testified before Congress in support of tax credits for adoptive families.

A couple from Kalamazoo, Michigan, adopted him when he was six weeks old. His adoptive mother died when he was five, and after that he moved from state to state as his adoptive father searched for work. The disruption in Thomas's young life helped drive him toward becoming an entrepreneur. As he grew up, he often sought refuge in work and in the friendly atmosphere of restaurants.

The success of Wendy's gave Thomas the ability to create programs to help children in situations similar to his. It gave him the power to make his foundation an active voice for the more than 100,000 children in the child welfare system who are waiting for homes and families. Some of these children are difficult to place because they are older, have a sibling they want to be adopted with, come from minority cultures, or are physically or mentally challenged.

The foundation supports adoption by raising awareness and by providing funding for other efforts that share Thomas's goals—making adoption affordable and increasing the number of North American children who are adopted in a timely way. It has distributed more than 500,000 copies of *The Beginner's Guide to Adoption*, a guide written by adoption experts for prospective adoptive parents. (This and other adoption resources are available on The National Adoption Foundation website.) It also promotes the creation of employee benefits programs to help adoptive parents. Wendy's was one of the first major corporations in America to provide employees who adopt with the same benefits as those who give birth. This includes extending the time off given to new mothers, called maternity leave, to parents of newly adopted children. In this way, Wendy's provides a model for other businesses throughout the nation.

Thomas often speaks out about adoption issues. He was a national spokesperson for "Adoption Works...For Everyone," a White House program when George Bush was president. He has also testified before Congress to support the idea that adoptive parents should get the same tax credits, or discounts on their taxes, that other parents are given for each child.

As the wealthy head of a corporation, Dave Thomas is able to support other causes that help children as well. He has contributed to St. Jude Children's Research Hospital in Memphis, Tennessee; the Children's Hospital in Columbus, Ohio; the Children's Home Society of Florida; and the Ohio State Cancer Research Institute.

WORKING TOWARD A BRIGHTER FUTURE

Ask successful people how they made it, and they'll often recall a person or place from their childhood that was an important factor in their success. Perhaps a special teacher or the staff at a local youth center gave them a chance to try different things and build their confidence. Many celebrities are working to give children today the same opportunities. They raise money for youth clubs that keep kids off the streets, help to develop community foundations that fund activities and scholarships that would not otherwise be available, and serve as role models. Their efforts are helping millions of disadvantaged children to believe in a bright future and set high goals for themselves.

★ *Denzel Washington* ★

Denzel Washington is an Academy Award-winning actor famous for his work in films such as *Malcolm X, Pelican Brief, Philadelphia,* and *Glory.* When he is not busy acting, he is also the national spokesperson for Boys & Girls Clubs of America, a nonprofit organization that teaches young people skills that will help them succeed in life. When Washington was a boy, his local Boys & Girls Club was like a second home to him, and he often says the experience helped him get where he is today.

The organization has grown since the first club opened in Hartford, Connecticut, in 1860. Today, there are 1,900 clubs in all 50 states, and in the U.S. Virgin Islands and Puerto Rico. There are 6,700 trained professionals on staff and 78,000 volunteers working with the 2.4 million boys and girls who are members.

Part of Washington's job as spokesperson is to tell people about his own life and inspire them to support the clubs. His father was a minister and his mother was a beautician, in his hometown of Mount Vernon, New York. Washington says he joined the club because he often saw children walking out from club meetings with smiles on their faces. Soon he was going there regularly for sports, parties, talent shows, and movies.

Denzel Washington credits the Boys & Girls Club with teaching him the importance of hard work, which helped him achieve success.

He also joined other club members for field trips—to New York City's Yankee Stadium, a planetarium, and different museums.

He learned the importance of hard work when he was on the club's relay team. "I was the slowest of the four runners, and when a new boy showed up, well, I was worried," Washington says of his experience. "My coach, who was always my mentor, was Billy Thomas. He said, 'This new boy doesn't have the foundation; he doesn't know the fundamentals, like how to run the corners and pass the baton.' The lesson Bill Thomas was teaching me was your natural ability will only take you so far."

The club's walls were covered with banners from colleges club members had gone on to attend, and that made Washington think about his future. "It was the first time I imagined far-off colleges and that I could possibly go to one," he remembered.

Washington went on to Fordham University in New York City to study journalism, then started pursuing his interest in the theater. Everyone said he had a natural acting ability, but he remembered Billy Thomas's words and decided that it was also important to learn the fundamentals of Shakespearean acting at the American Conservatory Theater in San Francisco.

In 1992, a childhood friend named David Belton contacted Washington to see if he would be interested in becoming involved with the Boys & Girls Clubs. The actor said yes, but that he wanted to do more than "just show up and shake hands." He began raising money and public awareness, touring the clubs, and meeting with reporters, and civic, business, and philanthropic leaders. He also appeared on national television to talk with Barbara Walters about the importance of the clubs.

Washington is not the only famous Boys & Girls Clubs graduate. The organization had a positive impact on President Bill Clinton, football player Randall Cunningham, newscaster Dan Rather, basketball player Shaquille O'Neal, boxer Sugar Ray Leonard, Olympian Jackie Joyner-Kersee, comedian Bill Cosby, and actor Robin Williams.

Washington feels the Boys & Girls Clubs serve an even more important purpose now than when he was a boy. He points out that young people today face difficult problems such as AIDS, drugs, gangs, and the breakup of families, and that kids need help finding companionship and a sense of belonging. In 1995, he conducted a club tour to raise awareness at both local and national levels. He started in Atlanta, Georgia, at the club's headquarters, then went on to Columbia, South Carolina, to dedicate a new club gymnasium. And in Pittsburgh, Pennsylvania, Washington addressed community leaders to promote the club as an alternative to gangs.

Denzel Washington sometimes stops in to visit a Boys & Girls Club and offer members encouragement when he is passing through a city. He tells kids he meets, "If you listen to the lessons taught here and apply yourself, with faith in God you will succeed. I promise you."

★ *Andrew Shue* ★

In 1993, Andrew Shue, who plays Billy on "Melrose Place," co-founded an organization called Do Something with his childhood friend, Michael Sanchez. Their mission is to offer support services to young people who are committed to improving their communities. One of their goals is to dispel the notion that the members of Generation X—the name for the generation of young people now in their 20s—don't care about making an impact on the world. Shue wants to bring their accomplishments into the public view.

The nonprofit organization operates on both national and local levels, providing young people with training, leadership courses, grant programs, and other support. The group emphasizes the belief that fundamental change occurs at the grass-roots, or local, level.

Shue was a community leader long before he became an actor. In high school, he was the student council president and started a program called Students Serving Seniors. The project matched students with senior citizens who needed help with chores and errands, or who simply needed some company. And later, after graduating from Dartmouth College, he traveled to Zimbabwe to teach math.

"It's really cool to come up with your own idea for…change and then watch it happen," Shue said in a 1994 interview for *Seventeen* magazine. "Somebody can come up to me and say, 'You did a great job on "Melrose Place," ' …and that feels good, but it goes away in about 30 seconds. But when you feel really fulfilled, then that's special, and I think it really affects your whole life. That's the best thing about service—it goes right to your soul."

As chairperson of the Do Something board of directors, Shue helps to run the organization, which operates out of a national office in New York City and has local offices in Newark, New Jersey; Boston, Massachusetts; and Washington, D.C. Each year, Shue helps select the winners of the Brick Awards, which Do Something gives to ten outstanding people in their teens and twenties who have launched programs to help their communities. The Brick Awards include a $100,000 grand prize and nine $10,000 prizes— money that recipients use to continue their work. Past winners have included Sean Closkey, who started a society that rehabilitates abandoned houses and sells them to low-income families, and Anthony Jones, who founded an organization to provide legal help to people in San Francisco who have been injured by law enforcement officers. Do Something also awards grants each year to help fund projects such as *X-press* magazine, which gives people in their twenties a voice.

Andrew Shue helps young people start community projects through Do Something.

In 1994, Michael J. Fox and George Stephanopolis celebrated the launching of Do Something's New York office with Andrew Shue.

Shue has made many appearances and given interviews for Do Something. He talked about the importance of the organization on the "Rosie O'Donnell Show" and, in 1995, helped host the first annual season finale Melrose Place/Beverly Hills 90210 fundraiser party. The event gave fans a chance to meet television stars while Do Something raised money and spread its message.

Many celebrities have pitched in to help Shue. In 1995, the Guess? company sold Do Something T-shirts and hosted in-store celebrity appearances by Shue, Dean Cain from "The New Adventures of Lois and Clark," Matt Fox from "Party of Five," Yasmine Bleeth from "Baywatch," Derek Harper from the New York Knicks, Rashaan Salaam from the Chicago Bears, and Tony Meola, goalkeeper for the U.S. World Cup Soccer team.

Shue hopes that Do Something will show young people that they can make a difference in their world. In a letter published in *Build*, the organization's magazine, he wrote, "My advice to all young people is to learn about the issues, work with others, and take action. Whether it is through Do Something or a program in your school, neighborhood, or community, everyone has a role to play."

Lynn Swann and Charlie Ward

Lynn Swann and Charlie Ward, two professional athletes, have made a difference in the lives of children and teenagers from needy families. Both men have committed themselves to Big Brothers Big Sisters of America, an organization that matches volunteer mentors with kids who need the support of an older friend.

Swann is the organization's national spokesperson and a member of the National Board of Directors. Between 1993 and 1995, he also served as president of the board. A 1981 National Football League Man of the Year, Swann was once described by sportscaster Howard Cosell as "maybe the most perfect wide receiver of his time." He was an All-American in football in his San Mateo, California, high school. He also played on two Rose Bowl teams while studying public relations at the University of Southern California. After he graduated, he was drafted by the Pittsburgh Steelers and helped the team win four Super Bowls before he retired from the game in 1983.

Swann later became a full-time broadcaster with ABC Sports, working on such events as the 1984 Summer Olympics, the Iditarod Trail Sled Dog Race, and "Monday Night Football."

Swann became involved with Big Brothers Big Sisters because he wanted to make a contribution to society. "I feel it is important for an individual to find out what they are most concerned about that is not working in our society, and then make an effort to change it for the best," he says.

As spokesperson for the organization, Swann has traveled across the United States and has visited the White House. He gives inspirational speeches that help raise money, inspire new volunteers, and educate people about the organization's work. At the 1996 Big Brothers Big Sisters of America National Conference in Washington, D.C., the former football player made a moving speech at a rally on Capitol Hill, urging listeners to encourage elected officials to support legislation that would improve opportunities for some of America's most vulnerable children.

Lynn Swann helps spread the word that the organization, founded in 1904, now has 500 agencies working with several million children in thousands of communities. The "big brothers" and "big sisters" who volunteer agree to spend several hours a week for at least a year with their "little brothers and sisters."

Lynn Swann feels that Big Brothers Big Sisters is an important positive influence in the lives of at-risk kids.

While Swann works for Big Brothers Big Sisters on the national level, Charlie Ward is the organization's spokesperson in Westchester County, New York. Selected in the first round of the National Basketball Association draft by the New York Knicks in 1994, the soft-spoken athlete also attracts attention because of his achievements in football. He was the first African-American quarterback at Florida State University and winner of the Heisman Trophy, which is given to the best collegiate football player in the country.

Ward volunteers as a "big brother" to Jourdan Francis, a nine-year-old from White Plains, New York. Ward's wife, Tonja, who is an attorney, acts as Jourdan's "big sister," and often shares a few hours with him when Ward is on the road with the Knicks. "We do all sorts of things together—fun things and educational stuff," Charlie Ward said during an interview about his relationship with Jourdan. "It's important that when we're together it's not just all fun and games. That's why we like to take Jourdan to museums or the library."

In addition to their work with Big Brothers Big Sisters of America, both Swann and Ward donate their time to other causes. In 1981, Swann created the Lynn Swann Youth Scholarship Fund in association with the Pittsburgh Ballet Theater School. This fund has helped provide close to 100 scholarships to children between the ages of 10 and 18 who have auditioned successfully to enter the school. Swann is also the national spokesperson for Project H.O.P.E., which teaches fifth- and sixth-grade students entrepreneurial skills.

Charlie Ward founded the "Guardian Ad Litem" basketball camp in Tallahassee, Florida. (*Guardian ad litem* is Latin and is the legal term for someone who protects the interests of a child in a

Charlie Ward is committed to his "little brother" Jourdan Francis.

court case.) The camp is a safe haven for physically and sexually abused children. He often makes guest appearances at churches and youth centers such as the Westchester County Center for Underprivileged Kids. In addition, Ward founded the Greyhound Shooting Stars Basketball Camp in Naugatuck, Connecticut. This camp provides children with the unique opportunity to learn about basketball from an expert.

But the two athletes are especially proud when they see how their work for Big Brothers Big Sisters is paying off. One study, targeting participants in New York City programs, showed that 84 percent of the young people in the program improved their performance in school within a year after they joined, 83 percent kept out of trouble, 90 percent improved relationships with friends, and 96 percent showed improved self-esteem. Through dedication and caring, Swann and Ward are helping children to improve their chances for a bright future.

★ Jackie Joyner-Kersee ★

Jackie Joyner-Kersee grew up in the ghetto in East St. Louis, Illinois, and started practicing the long jump as a teenager. Although she didn't know it at the time, she was destined to be part of a family of track-and-field stars. Her brother, Al, won a gold medal in the triple jump at the 1984 Olympics. He married Delorez Florence Griffith, a sprint champion who earned three Olympic gold medals. Jackie became an accomplished heptathlete (an athlete who competes in a contest that includes seven events) and long jumper, and she won gold medals in the 1987 World Championships, the 1988 Olympics, and the 1992 Olympics.

To Joyner-Kersee, such tremendous success meant that she would be able to give kids back in her hometown the kinds of opportunities that had helped her believe in herself. When Joyner-Kersee was a girl in East St. Louis, she lived around the corner from the Mary Brown Center for Youth. She read in the library at the center, learned crafts, and took part in cheerleading and modern dance activities. She also got her first job there—she ran errands for the center supervisor. As an adult, her goal is to provide similar opportunities for the kids who live in East St. Louis today.

In 1989, she established the Jackie Joyner-Kersee Community Foundation. This foundation provides scholarships to worthy students and honors African-American community leaders such as Theodore "Pop" Myles, an East St. Louis teacher and security guard who was a positive role model for many of the children in that area. When Joyner-Kersee retired from Olympic competition in 1996, she moved from Los Angeles, where she had been living, back to East St. Louis so that she could be more involved in making positive changes there.

In that same year, the athlete began her newest project. She and her foundation joined forces with business and civic leaders from the East St. Louis metropolitan area to create the Jackie Joyner-Kersee Youth Center Foundation. Their goal is to build a center that will be available to people of all ages and provide special activities for at least 6,000 young people a year. Joyner-Kersee wants to offer young people jobs at the center and to work with corporations in St. Louis, Illinois, to create more job opportunities in the greater metropolitan area. She also wants to get kids involved in activities such as scouting, art, and music. Her center will be very much like the Mary Brown Center—an

Jackie Joyner-Kersee is giving East St. Louis kids the opportunity to learn, work, and grow through her community organization.

alternative to the streets, and a place for youth to learn community responsibility, morals, and values. By creating jobs and bringing a new spirit of enthusiasm into East St. Louis, Joyner-Kersee hopes to help provide a better future for the families in that area who live in poverty.

Joyner-Kersee and her supporters are working to raise $12.5 million, partly by getting corporations, individuals, and organizations in East St. Louis and around the country to make pledges. They expect to be able to start building by 1998.

Eventually, the center will contain indoor sport courts and locker rooms, baseball and football fields, a track-and-field stadium, a wellness center, education rooms, a library, a computer laboratory, an indoor recreation center with a pool, and a performing arts center. The wellness center will have a full-time nurse who will provide immunizations, and teach young people about nutrition, disease prevention, and other health topics. Classes offered in the education rooms will supplement what kids learn in school, covering such topics as music and computers.

Some celebrities put their modest roots behind them once they become successful. Jackie Joyner-Kersee's efforts, however, have won her praise in her hometown for remembering where she came from. She told *Good Housekeeping*, "I'm always on the road and hardly ever see my family and friends. But they understand, and when I do see them, their comment to me is always, 'Jackie, you haven't changed a bit!'"

★ A.C. Green ★

A.C. Green is 6'9" tall and stands out in a crowd. His height is an advantage in basketball, where he is known as one of the hardest working players on the court. A collegiate star player for the Oregon State Beavers, Green's professional career began when he was drafted by the Los Angeles Lakers in 1985. He later played for the Phoenix Suns before he was traded to the Dallas Mavericks in 1997. By the fall of that year, Green had played 900 consecutive games and on November 20, 1997, he broke basketball star Randy Smith's 906-game record—known as the "NBA Iron Man" streak. He was selected by fans as a starter in the 1990 NBA All-Star Game and was named to the NBA All-Defensive second team in 1989.

In addition to being a great athlete, Green has started a number of programs to benefit society under the umbrella of A.C. Green Programs for Youth.

One of these programs is called Athletes for Abstinence. (Abstinence means to refrain from having sexual intercourse.) Its mission is to prevent pregnancy and sexually transmitted diseases by encouraging people to practice abstinence before marriage. The program offers a video called *It Ain't Worth It*, which features athletes who discuss why they have chosen abstinence, and a six-week curriculum for students ages 12 to 18, called "I've Got the Power." It teaches young people that they have power over their own bodies and lives.

Green is quoted in Athletes for Abstinence literature as saying, "Everyone won't believe in the things that I believe. I try and respect them, and at the same time I hope they can respect what I believe.... Abstinence is the only true form of safe sex."

Another of the A.C. Green Programs for Youth is the Youth Leadership Camp that helps inner city kids in the Los Angeles,

Through his programs, A.C. Green encourages kids to believe in themselves and to make the most of their lives.

California; Phoenix, Arizona; and Portland, Oregon, areas. Every summer, this basketball camp hosts about 130 boys and girls between the ages of 9 and 15 for three sessions, each one week long. Many of the campers are children who have been physically or emotionally abused, are homeless, or are growing up in broken families. At the camp, they play basketball, explore career ideas, learn self-esteem, and build their confidence. Green personally supervises the camp and talks to the young people about how a sense of purpose can make a difference in their lives.

Green has another program, currently in development, called Career Move. This project will provide young people with internships (jobs in which students work in exchange for the opportunity to acquire skills), training programs, and exposure to a variety of careers. It urges participants to think about what they want to do in five years, encourages them to dream, and teaches them to plan.

Green's celebrity status is a powerful tool in raising money for good causes. He charges $7,500 for personal appearances and speaking engagements, and donates this money to his youth foundation. He also helps raise money for other organizations dedicated to helping kids by autographing items and donating them. These items are auctioned off at various fund-raising events. A.C. Green is one athlete who has made a big impact both on and off the court.

Even athletes who put off college to pursue their sports seem to agree that education is one of the keys to a good life. Many celebrities have helped with publicity campaigns for organizations that promote reading and learning. Some have started camps and other programs where young people can explore educational paths and career options that they might not have thought about otherwise. Others sponsor contests or host pizza dinners—imaginative activities that show children that learning can be fun.

OFFERING THE GIFT OF KNOWLEDGE

★ *Shaquille O'Neal* ★

Shaquille O'Neal, affectionately called "Shaq," is 7 feet tall, weighs 350 pounds, and has made as much as $20 million a year playing basketball. He first became a star on the court playing ball, for the Orlando Magic from 1992 to 1996 and then for the Los Angeles Lakers. Children also know him as the good genie in the 1996 Disney film *Kazaam*.

O'Neal is known for his spontaneous generosity. Sometimes he drives through poor neighborhoods bearing gifts. He likes to pick out a house where kids live and walk in with a new television set. If the family accepts the gift, he'll sit down and watch a few shows with the kids. "I was taught by my parents to help people, period," he told reporters a few years ago at the dedication of a playground he helped restore in Newark, New Jersey, where his grandmother lives.

So, when the National Basketball Association decided to support the literacy outreach efforts of the largest American children's literacy organization, Reading Is Fundamental (RIF), O'Neal volunteered to become national spokesperson for the group.

RIF is a nonprofit organization that reaches out to almost 4 million children of all ages in 50 states, the District of Columbia, Puerto Rico, the U.S. Virgin Islands, and Guam. RIF's 219,000 volunteers run more than 5,700 projects at 18,000 locations. They organize many reading activities like the MetLife-sponsored National Reading Celebration, where kids are challenged to meet or exceed a personal reading goal. The organization also gives free books to more than three million children a year.

O'Neal frequently attends RIF events, where he has told children, "The more you know how to read, the more you can get things accomplished. You can't fill out a job application if you

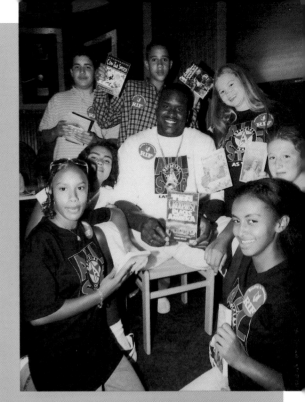

While in Las Vegas, in June 1997, Shaquille O'Neal met with RIF kids from the Orr Middle School.

can't read. And if you can't fill out a job application, then you can't get a job." He considers reading and education so important that, even though he is successful as a basketball player, he went back to Louisiana State University to finish earning his college degree.

Knowing that Shaq is big on books, RIF and the NBA asked him to appear in a televised public announcement. In it, he visits a library where he finds children reading classic books whose titles have been given a twist on his name, such as "Little Shaq Horner" and "Shaq and the Beanstalk." O'Neal also promoted a sweepstakes for RIF in which children wrote about each book they read over the summer to become eligible to win tickets to an Orlando Magic game, along with airline tickets and hotel accommodations.

Other celebrities who have participated in RIF activities include NBA stars Juwan Howard, Danny Manning, Reggie Miller, Tim Hardaway, John Stockton, Hakeem Olajuwon, and Grant Hill. Some have made public service announcements and have helped with projects such as READ BIG, which challenged second and third graders to read 100 books and rewarded those who succeeded with NBA school supplies.

O'Neal and other NBA players enjoy working for RIF because it reminds them of when they first became interested in reading. Some of them have even compiled a list of their favorite childhood books. John Amaechi, who plays for Cleveland, liked *The Hardy Boys Mysteries*, Nat McMillan, who plays for Seattle, enjoyed *Green Eggs and Ham*, and O'Neal says one of his favorite books was *Curious George*.

RIF is only one of many causes that O'Neal supports. When he lived in Orlando, he donated tickets to Magic home games to underprivileged youths, gave Christmas presents to needy kids, and sent Valentine's Day roses to women in Orlando hospitals. He also helped serve an annual Thanksgiving dinner to homeless men, women, and children sponsored by the Coalition for the Homeless of Central Florida in Orlando. One year, he read Tomie dePaola's picture book, *My First Thanksgiving*, aloud to children who came to the dinner, and RIF distributed free books to the children as mementos of the occasion. Now that he lives in Los Angeles, he brings this "Shaqsgiving" tradition to the Watts Labor Community Action Council there.

Once, speaking with a reporter from *Build* magazine, Shaquille O'Neal said, "I realize that I am a role model...I realize that there are children who look up to me." He takes his responsibility as a celebrity very seriously.

★ *Mariah Carey* ★

Mariah Carey began writing songs at the age of 13. By the time she was 25, she was a phenomenon in pop music, and her voice had soared around the world. She had sold more than 55 million albums, recorded five consecutive Number One hits, won two Grammy Awards, and appeared in several television specials. Even in the midst of such success, however, there was something else she wanted to do. She said, "I had the idea to start a summer camp to try to make a difference in the lives of city kids."

Carey knew about the obstacles some kids face, because she'd had a tough time growing up herself. She was born in New York City, and her parents divorced when she was three. After that, she moved with her mother from one place to another. Other children criticized her for her striking looks, the result of her Venezuelan-African-Irish heritage.

When Carey researched her summer camp idea, she discovered an organization called the Fresh Air Fund that was already doing exactly what she envisioned. The Fresh Air Fund has four camps in Fishkill, New York, amid 3,000 acres of hilly land with lakes, ponds, streams, and hiking trails. More than 2,500 inner city kids a year attend these camps and can swim, study the stars, and see deer and other wildlife in their natural environment. The four camps are Camp Anita Bliss Coler for young girls, Camp Hayden-Marks Memorial for young boys, Camp Pioneer for teenage boys, and Camp Hidden Valley, a co-ed camp for teenage boys and girls, including those who are disabled.

The Fresh Air Fund was founded in 1877 by a New York City clergyman who took children out of the rundown tenements of the city to visit the homes and farms of country folk, and it has since helped 1.6 million children. Besides sending young people to camp, the Fresh Air Fund has also placed 7,000 children a year in private homes for two-week stays with families in 13 states from Maine to Virginia and in Canada.

When Carey contacted administrators at the Fresh Air Fund and told them how interested she was in their organization, she was asked to be its lifetime spokesperson. Carey agreed in late 1994, and quickly got involved with a special project for the group. She committed $1 million to help support a new career-oriented camp. Organizers decided to name the camp after her.

Since then, Carey has devoted both time and money to Camp Mariah, located on the banks of a 50-acre lake in Fishkill. The camp provides career information and camping experiences every summer for 300 boys and girls ages 12 to 15, as well as year-round activities in New York City. It's a place where young people can assess their strengths, practice critical thinking, and learn interpersonal skills. Opportunities such as a career fair, and a chance to work with volunteer mentors are provided. Doctors, lawyers, scientists, and other professionals visit the camp to talk about the work they do and how they prepared for their careers.

In addition, Carey often drops in at the camp to talk about employment opportunities in the music industry. She has said

Mariah Carey celebrated the opening of the Fresh Air Fund's Camp Mariah in August 1996.

that she wants to encourage children to follow their dreams. "My mother always told me I could be whatever I wanted to be if I kept at it and really believed in myself. But other people didn't give me the same encouragement. I told one teacher that I wanted to be a singer and was told, 'There are millions of people out there who can sing. What makes you any different? Don't get your hopes up.' I couldn't believe a teacher would actually say that to someone who had a dream."

Mariah Carey held on to her positive attitude, and it paid off. She later wrote a song called "Hero" that tells of believing in and relying on oneself. It became one of her biggest hits. The hope at Camp Mariah is that young people there will learn to have the same confidence as Carey, so that they too can grow up to be whatever they want to be.

★ *Scottie Pippen* ★

Scottie Pippen is a professional basketball player who has helped lead the Chicago Bulls to several championships. Pippen is also a two-time Olympian and one of the National Basketball Association's top 50 players. While it would be easy to be overshadowed by such famous teammates as Michael Jordan and Dennis Rodman, he has won a reputation as a great athlete.

Pippen was the youngest of 13 children growing up in rural Hamburg, Arkansas. From a young age, he wanted to do what he could to support his community and give people an easier life. Becoming a famous basketball player has given him the opportunity to do this, and he has made a difference in the lives of thousands of people. He founded the Scottie Pippen Youth Foundation in 1992, which benefits underprivileged youths in Chicago, Illinois, and in Arkansas. One of the activities of the foundation is to hold charitable basketball games between professional NBA athletes in Chicago and Little Rock, Arkansas, to raise money for the foundation. The funds raised are used for such projects as the donation of 500 winter coats every Christmas to kids in Chicago's Cabrini-Green housing projects.

The foundation also commits financial support and Pippen gives his time to the Cabrini-Green Tutoring Program. This program was started in 1965 by a group of employees from the Montgomery Ward company who tutored youths in the Cabrini-Green housing projects. People who live in these projects are plagued by a 70 percent high school drop-out rate, so the tutoring program now provides one-on-one help to 450 students in the hopes that they will graduate. The program's mission is "to stimulate children's desire to learn through lessons and to develop self-esteem and friendships with adult role models."

Pippen goes out of his way to be a role model by visiting with young people in the Cabrini-Green program. In 1995, he sponsored a Scottie Pippen Reading Contest, offering prizes to the more than 80 kids who participated. He also invited the 33 winners to join him for pizza at Moretti's Restaurant in Chicago and signed each one's favorite book. Then they all attended a Chicago Bulls game together and watched the team win their 68th game that season.

Scottie Pippen also contributes to other causes, including the Big Brothers Big Sisters of America, the Fellowship of

Scottie Pippen poses with two children from the Cabrini-Green Tutoring Program who took part in the Scottie Pippen Reading Contest.

At an event in 1995, Pippen played basketball and gave out free athletic shoes, rewarding kids from Cabrini-Green who had perfect school attendance and good behavior.

Christian Athletes Sports Camps in Arkansas, and the Arkansas Children's Hospital in Little Rock. But he is especially proud of his own foundation, which pitches in whenever it can to help children and others in need. Along with helping young people at Cabrini-Green, the foundation has helped to fund *Streetwise* (a newspaper created by and for the homeless of Chicago), donated hundreds of fans to the elderly during a deadly Chicago heat wave, and sent $25,000 to the children of the victims of the famous federal building bombing in Oklahoma City. After the bombing, Pippen was quoted as saying, "It's times like this that remind us just how small the game of basketball is."

Children in countries around the world are living in tragic situations. Many wake up every day to face poverty, famine, disease, or war. Some celebrities who have traveled to various parts of the world and witnessed these huge problems firsthand have committed themselves to educating politicians and others about the plight of these children. In many cases, these celebrities are directly or indirectly providing children in need with such necessities as food, shelter, and medicine—in other words, they are saving lives.

REACHING OUT TO THE CHILDREN OF THE WORLD

★ *Harry Belafonte* ★

Harry Belafonte is a legend in the music world. In 1955, he sparked an international calypso music craze as his record album, "Calypso," became the first album in history to sell over a million copies. In 1985, he brought together 45 top performers to record the hit song, "We Are the World," which raised millions of dollars for emergency assistance needed in Africa.

Respected not only as a musician but also as an entertainer and a humanitarian, Belafonte's list of achievements includes a Tony Award, an Emmy Award, and several movie roles. As a social activist, he was a major force in the Civil Rights Movement, the battle against racial inequality in America; and in the struggle against apartheid, the policy of strict racial segregation that divided South Africa. President John F. Kennedy appointed him as the first entertainer to serve as cultural advisor to the Peace Corps, a U.S. government agency that sends volunteers to help people in developing countries.

But one of his greatest accomplishments in life has been making a powerful difference in helping children in need all over the world. He does this through the United Nations International Children's

Emergency Fund (UNICEF), the branch of the United Nations that supports children in developing nations. Established in 1945, UNICEF was originally responsible for assisting child welfare programs in countries devastated by World War II. In 1950, it expanded its scope to help children in developing nations with child nutrition, health and welfare programs, and food and medical supplies in emergencies.

UNICEF Goodwill Ambassador Harry Belafonte travels extensively to educate people about the needs of children.

Belafonte has worked with UNICEF as a Goodwill Ambassador since 1987. He has traveled all over the world for the organization and supported it through benefit concerts, television specials, fund-raising events, and by speaking out for children—using his unique voice to call attention to their plights.

According to UNICEF, 12.4 million children die each year—largely from causes that could be prevented. UNICEF is helping children survive by supporting and improving community-based services in health care, education, and sanitation in more than 140 developing countries.

When UNICEF Executive Director James P. Grant appointed Belafonte as a Goodwill Ambassador, the entertainer left almost immediately for his first mission. He traveled to Dakar, Senegal, to serve as chair of the International Symposium of Artists and Intellectuals for African Children. Belafonte used the symposium, a gathering at which people exchange ideas, to spread the message that it is possible to save millions of children from dying, for example, just by making sure they have safe water to drink. He also brought media attention to the event by performing his music along with more than 20 other artists in a huge concert.

During a 1994 trip to Rwanda, Harry Belafonte helps transport Rwandan children to a refugee camp for youngsters who are orphaned or who have been separated from their parents.

In Senegal, Belafonte also witnessed that country's third vaccination drive, which resulted in the protection of 75 percent of the country's children from disease.

A year later, he was in Africa again, at a second symposium jointly sponsored by the Zimbabwe Committee for Child Survival and UNICEF, called Children on the Frontline. Belafonte headed the symposium's organizing committee and took part in another major concert with top artists. He was instrumental in arranging for all of the artists to donate any profits they received for their performances or for TV and video releases of the concert so that any income could go directly to benefiting children.

Belafonte has continued to travel extensively for UNICEF, educating the world about children who are suffering. In Mozambique, the media followed him to a special school for children who had suffered terribly at the hands of politically motivated kidnappers. In the Netherlands, in 1988, he was a guest on "The Danny Kaye Awards Show," which raised more than $2.5 million for UNICEF-assisted programs. In the United States, he hosted a huge rally in New York City's Central Park for the UNICEF 1990 World Summit for Children, a conference that addressed issues affecting children around the world.

Many organizations have recognized Belafonte for his dedicated work. Over the last several years, he has received honors from such diverse groups as the Variety Club women (the world's largest volunteer children's charity), the American Jewish Congress, and the National Association for the Advancement of Colored People. In 1994, just after Belafonte and his wife, Julie, had returned from another UNICEF mission to Rwanda, President Clinton invited him to a special White House ceremony. There, Belafonte was presented with one of the nation's highest honors—the National Medal of the Arts.

While philanthropic work takes up a lot of his time, Harry Belafonte likes to take breaks at home in New York City, spending time with his wife, children, and grandchildren. Now in his 70s, he is still a popular entertainer, appearing in new films and singing in concerts. But, in 1996, when a reporter for *Ebony* magazine asked him how he would like to be remembered, he said nothing about being rich or famous. He explained that the pursuit of "power and money is a remarkable waste of a life. I would like in the end for it to be understood that he put his life in service."

★ *Tom Chapin* ★

Tom Chapin has been recording music for children for more than 20 years. His brother, Harry Chapin, was also a folk singer and social activist who was killed in an automobile accident in 1981. Influenced by such famous folk singers as Pete Seeger and Woody Guthrie, Tom Chapin is a talented songwriter. He has written lyrics for children about everything from riding the bus to what people around the world eat for dinner.

Tom Chapin and collaborators John Forster and Michael Mark began writing and recording such kids' songs as "Family Tree," "Moonboat," "Mother Earth," "Billy the Squid," and "Zig Zag" in the early 1980s. They knew the songs were a success when teachers said they were using them in classrooms, when parents said they took Chapin's tapes on long car trips, and when children who came to his concerts already knew the words to the songs.

For Chapin, his purpose as a musician was becoming clear. "This is the media age, and kids get a lot of bad news," Chapin said in an interview with *Billboard* magazine. "My job is to spread good news."

Spreading good news to children who live in poverty can be a difficult job. So Chapin does what he can for them through Save the Children,

Singer Tom Chapin is always looking for new ways to help Save the Children in their mission to bring aid to children around the world.

an organization based in Connecticut. Save the Children was established in 1932 by a group of concerned citizens who wanted to help families in poor areas during the Great Depression. Today, the organization helps millions of children in the United States and in 39 other countries. It provides children with food and shelter, protects them during times of war, and offers medical services. One of its primary goals is to work with communities on long-term projects that ensure the health and survival of children. It has been instrumental in thousands of efforts to help the needy, from the development and distribution of a "Safe Birthing Kit" that has saved the lives of new mothers and infants, to early education programs that help children growing up in the midst of war in the Balkans experience more normal childhoods.

Chapin had known about the organization for years before his record company suggested he find a way to work with it. He knew that anyone can sponsor a needy child by sending a regular donation each month, and he decided to sponsor two children. One of the children he sponsors lives in Chile and the other is in Zaire.

In addition, Chapin found a way to use his musical talents to support the organization. If you were to buy a copy of his "Around the World and Back Again" CD, you would find a Save the Children sticker on its cover. There is a card inside the CD with a phone number for the Save the Children Kids' Club, which provides children with information about helping other kids around the world. The CD features musical styles from such varied places as Managua, Nicaragua, and Saskatoon, Canada, and includes a song called "Heartache to Happy," which was chosen as a theme song for Save the Children.

Chapin also talks about the mission of the organization at his concerts and invites Save the Children volunteers to set up booths there so that concertgoers can obtain more information. In addition, he appears in a televised public service announcement for the group.

Tom Chapin is a family man who loves children. He lives in Rockland County, New York, with his wife, Bonnie, and their two daughters, Abigail and Lily. He also has two stepchildren, Jonathan and Jessica. In addition to his work for Save the Children, Chapin continues the work of his late brother Harry as a member of the board of directors for World Hunger Year (WHY)—a New York-based educational organization that Harry Chapin founded in 1975. WHY fights hunger through its support of grass-roots organizations that deal with the problems of hunger at a local level. It also serves as an information source about these problems.

In an interview in the *Tampa Tribune* newspaper, Chapin said it is important to give something back to the world. His contributions have come naturally in the course of his life and his work. He summed up his feelings by saying, "You should live your life as if it matters."

Celebrities Who CARE

Lloyd Bridges has been a famous actor for many years. During his 40-year career on screen, he faced man-eating sharks, western gun-slingers, and Nazi troops. He starred in the popular television series "Sea Hunt" and the classic movie *High Noon*.

Bridges says that one of his most difficult roles, however, has been as a volunteer for the Cooperative for Assistance and Relief Everywhere (CARE), one of the world's largest international relief and development organizations. CARE has attracted the interest of dozens of celebrities. The list includes such people as singer Mary Chapin Carpenter and comedian Whoopi Goldberg.

Bridges is one of many committed volunteers who works for CARE. He has traveled abroad for the organization and witnessed real-life dramas that are often very sad. On a trip to Ethiopia in 1988, the poorest country he had ever visited, he met a woman whose husband had just died. The woman was standing with hundreds of other people waiting for a food allotment, holding her starving son in her arms. "Suddenly the whole thing hit me," Bridges said, upon his return to the United States. "I cried. Nobody wants to see anyone die of hunger."

Lloyd Bridges helped with CARE's Agricultural/Food Security Project during his trip to Ethiopia in 1988.

CARE was established more than 50 years ago to give Americans a reliable way to play a personal role in rebuilding war-ravaged Europe after World War II. It has since helped more than one billion children and adults in developing nations in Africa, Asia, Latin America, and eastern Europe. The organization now has 10,000 staff people working long days under difficult, often dangerous conditions to provide emergency relief and programs that help people take control of their environment, economic survival, health care, and education.

Bridges has served as a special agent for CARE, witnessing events in poverty-stricken countries and informing CARE about the situations. In 1988, he toured CARE emergency food distribution centers and community development projects in Ethiopia and Kenya when those nations were suffering from severe drought. His fame caused the trip to be covered by reporters from the Associated Press and the *New York Times*, which helped draw attention to the desperate need for aid to those nations. Then Bridges went home to tell Americans exactly what he saw and to urge them to help CARE make a difference. He conducted interviews with the "Today Show," *USA Today*, "Showbiz Tonight," the *New York Daily News*, the *New York Post*, *Newsday*, "Larry King Live," and "The Morning Show."

Bridges and his wife, Dorothy, both received special Humanitarian Awards in 1992 from CARE for their trip, as well as for financial and other support that they have given to CARE over the years. Recently, their son, actor Beau Bridges, was one of the celebrities filmed for a CARE television appeal. (Their other son, actor Jeff Bridges, founded an anti-hunger group called End Hunger Network.)

Several years after the Bridges's African trip, Mary Chapin Carpenter became involved with CARE. A singer and songwriter who has won five Grammy Awards, she grew up in a family that traveled around the world and saw children suffering in places such as Delhi, India.

When Howard Schultz, the head of Starbucks coffee, a major corporate supporter of CARE, offered to sponsor Chapin Carpenter's 70-city "Stones in the Road" tour and suggested using the tour to promote CARE, she was interested in the idea. She arranged to talk about CARE to her audiences, have CARE information booths set up at her concerts, and donate proceeds from the sales of the tour program to the organization. She also included a message about CARE's work and a request for support in the liner notes of her CD, "Stones in the Road." Chapin Carpenter talked about CARE's mission on a CD-ROM sampler that features ten musicians, and did a voice-over for the CARE website.

Mary Chapin Carpenter has brought a lot of attention to CARE through her concert tour.

(In addition to her work for CARE, she recorded a lullaby collection for children called "Till Their Eyes Shine." Sales of the collection benefit the Voiceless Victims Project of the Institute for Intercultural Understanding in Louisville, Kentucky. This project researches and documents the effects on children of conflict, war, and violence through the children's artwork and poetry.)

Other supporters of CARE include movie stars Robert DeNiro, Marlee Matlin, and Louis Gossett, Jr. Whoopi Goldberg has donated money and time, appearing in a public service advertising campaign that helped CARE celebrate its 50th anniversary in 1995.

Many say they have been touched by what they see in countries where CARE is helping. Upon his return from Ethiopia, Lloyd Bridges said, "We saw people who have been beaten down by war, by drought and by poverty. But nowhere did we see anyone who has given up hope." Bridges hopes he and other celebrities can assist CARE in helping families around the world to build a better future for their children.

★ ★

The celebrities in this book have dedicated themselves to making a difference in the lives of children. Many have used their names to raise millions of dollars and attract attention to the plights of children who are underprivileged, orphaned, or abused. Some regularly spend time with children in need of support, taking them to movies or sports events, and providing them with alternatives to life on the streets. Others have traveled all over the world to visit children who have suffered through war or famine. All of these celebrities have given an impressive amount of time, money, and energy, and they have indeed made a difference. Because of their good work, more children are living better lives and facing brighter futures.

Glossary

activist A person who believes in, and actively supports, a cause.

advocacy The act of speaking or writing in support of a cause.

entrepreneur A person who spends time and/or money pursuing business opportunities for himself or herself.

foundation An organization established to provide financial and other assistance to institutions or projects.

fund-raiser An event that raises money for a charity or other interest.

grant Money from a fund given to help further a cause.

grass-roots movement A movement, usually local, that begins among ordinary people as opposed to movements connected with political parties or other large organizations.

internship Period of unpaid service by a person, usually a student, who is still learning.

mentor A supportive person who serves as a teacher, coach, or advisor.

outreach An effort to extend assistance or services to those who need them.

philanthropy The giving of money or time in order to benefit a cause.

public service announcement An announcement on TV, radio, or other medium designed to educate or give information to the public.

Further Reading

Chandler, Gary and Kevin Graham. *Celebrity Activists: Environmental Causes.* New York: Twenty-First Century Books, 1997.

Glaser, Elizabeth and Timothy L. Biel. *The Ethiopian Famine.* San Diego, CA: Lucent Books, 1990.

Lewis, Barbara A. *The Kid's Guide to Service Projects: Over 500 Service Ideas for Young People Who Want to Make a Difference.* Minneapolis, MN: Free Spirit Publishers, 1995.

O'Connor, Karen. *Homeless Children.* San Diego, CA: Lucent Books, 1992.

Pippen, Scottie and Greg Brown. *Reach Higher.* Dallas, TX: Taylor Publishing, 1997.

Stone, Tanya Lee. *Celebrity Activists: Medical Causes.* New York: Twenty-First Century Books, 1997.

For More Information

A.C. Green Programs for Youth can be reached at (800) AC-YOUTH or on the Internet at http://www.acgreen.com

Big Brothers Big Sisters of America, 230 North 13th Street, Philadelphia, PA 19107, or on the Internet at http://www.bbbsa.org/

Boys & Girls Clubs of America, 1230 West Peachtree Street NW, Atlanta, GA 30309, or on the Internet at http://www.bgca.org/

CARE, 151 Ellis Street NE, Atlanta, GA 30303-2439, or on the Internet at http://www.care.org/

Childhelp USA, 15757 North 78 Street, Scottsdale, AZ 85260, (602) 922-8212, or on the Internet at http://www.childhelpusa.org

Dave Thomas Foundation for Adoption is on the Internet at http://nac.adopt.org/wendy.html

And information about the adoption process and a comprehensive list of resources is available through an online version of "Adoption Works...for Everyone" at http://www.wendys.com/rdavidf.htm

Do Something, 423 West 55th Street, 8th Floor, New York, NY 10019. They can also be reached on America Online by typing the keyword: Do Something, or on the Internet at http://www.dosomething.org Free subscriptions to *Build* are available.

Fresh Air Fund, 1040 Avenue of the Americas, Third Floor, New York, NY 10018, or on the Internet at http://www.freshair.org/

National Adoption Center, 1500 Walnut Street, Suite 701, Philadelphia, PA 19102, or on the Internet at http://nac.adopt.org/

Reading Is Fundamental, 600 Maryland Avenue SW, Suite 600, Washington, D.C. 20024, or on the Internet at http://www.si.edu/rif

Save the Children, 54 Wilton Road, Westport, CT 06880, (800) 243-5075, or on the Internet at http://www.savethechildren.org/

UNICEF, The U.S. Committee for UNICEF, 333 East 38th Street, New York, NY 10016, (800) FOR-KIDS, or on the Internet at http://www.unicef.org/

Index

Photo Credits

Cover: PhotoDisk, Inc.; page 8: courtesy of The Greenwich House; page 11: courtesy of Childhelp USA; page 14: ©Garo Lachinian/SABA; page 17: courtesy of the Christopher Zorich Foundation, pages 20, 30, 34: AP/Wide World Photos; page 24: ©Fortin-Neifer/Action Press/SABA; pages 27, 28, 45: ©Kevin Mazur; page 32: courtesy of the Terrie Williams Agency; page 37: courtesy of A.C. Green Programs for Youth; pages 47, 48: courtesy of the Cabrini-Green Tutoring Program; pages 51, 52: courtesy of UNICEF; page 55: courtesy of Save the Children; pages 58, 59: courtesy of CARE.